The Perfect Pet Shop

Vivian French

Illustrated by
Selina Young

Orion
Children's Books

for Port Ellen Primary School, Islay,
with love

The stories from *The Perfect Pet Shop* originally appeared in
The Story House first published in Great Britain in 2004
by Orion Children's Books
This edition first published in 2012
by Orion Children's Books
a division of the Orion Publishing Group Ltd
Orion House
5 Upper St Martin's Lane
London WC2H 9EA
An Hachette UK Company

Text copyright © Vivian French 2004 and 2012
Illustrations copyright © Selina Young 2004
Designed by Louise Millar

The right of Vivian French and Selina Young
to be identified as the author and illustrator
respectively of this work has been asserted.

A catalogue record for this book is available
from the British Library

Printed and bound in China

ISBN 978 1 4440 0514 1

Contents

The Perfect Pet Shop

Mr Peter's Perfect Pet Shop was closed for the night. Mr Peter was at home, fast asleep, but the animals were wide awake.

"Woof! Woof!" The little white puppy was running round his cage. "Isn't this fun? Hello, guinea pigs! Where are your tails? Hello, rabbit!"

"Sssh!" The rabbit held up a paw. "Be quiet, puppy! Don't you know it's bedtime?"

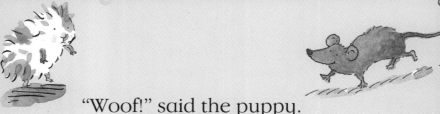

"Woof!" said the puppy.
"Bedtime? But I'm not sleepy!"

"Eek, squeak!" said the little
white mouse. "Such a noise! Mice
are **never** noisy."

"Yes you are," said the puppy.
"My mum told me a story about a
very noisy mouse!"

The mouse looked cross, but the
rabbit came closer. "'If we let you
tell us your story, will you go to
sleep afterwards?"

"Yes," said the puppy.

"Go on then," said the guinea
pigs. "Tell us the story!"

When William and Mimi Came to Stay

Once there was a house, and in
the house there was a hallway.
In the hallway was a mousehole,
and in the mousehole lived Ferdie
and his mum. Ferdie's cousins
were coming to stay.

Ferdie was very excited.

"They live in the country," his mum told him. "They'll be quiet little mice."

Scritch … scritch … scritch.

There was a teeny weeny scratching on Ferdie's front door.

"They're here!" shouted Ferdie.

Bang! Bang!

The mousehole shook.

Mum opened the door, and found two teeny weeny mice on the doorstep.

"It's William and Mimi!" she said.

William rushed in and hid under a cushion.

Mimi stayed on the doorstep.

"Hello!" she said.

Ferdie put his paws over his ears. Mimi had the loudest voice he had ever heard.

"We've seen a big furry animal with long white whiskers," Mimi went on. "It was asleep. It went purrrrr!"

Ferdie's mum shut the door and locked it.

"Oh, Mimi!" she said. "That was the cat! Cats eat mice!"

"Oh … oh … oh … " wailed
William. "I don't like it here!"

"Poor William," said Ferdie's
mum. "Don't worry. Ferdie will
look after you when you go out."

William began to tremble.
"I don't want to go out!"

Mimi jumped up and down.
"Out?" she shouted. "Can
we go now?"

Ferdie stared at Mimi. She really was very tiny.

"Was it you who went bang bang on our door?" he asked.

"Yes." Mimi looked proud. "William's quiet. I'm noisy."

Ferdie's mum sat down on the sofa. "Mimi," she said. "How long are you staying?"

"I think we should go home now," whispered William.

"We can stay for a week," Mimi bellowed.

That afternoon Ferdie's mum had a headache.

"Shall I take Mimi and William out?" Ferdie asked.

Mimi jumped up. "I'm ready!" she said. "Come on, William!"

But William wouldn't come. He said he'd rather do the dusting.

"I'll make Aunty Mouse a cup of tea," he whispered.

"Thank you, dear," said Ferdie's mum.

"Sh," said Ferdie as he and Mimi
tiptoed out of the mousehole.

Crash!

Mimi slammed the front door.

"Meow?" The cat woke up.
Ferdie pushed Mimi under the
hall cupboard.

The cat stretched. Then it began
sniffing up and down the hallway.

"I told you to be quiet!" Ferdie whispered crossly. "Don't move!"

Mimi nodded, and the two little mice stayed very still.

At last the cat padded away.

"Phew!" said Ferdie.

"Can we find some cheese?" Mimi asked.

"No," Ferdie said. "We're going home." They hurried out from under the cupboard – and stopped.

The big grey cat was crouching in front of the mousehole.

Ferdie and Mimi could see the
his claws. They looked very sharp.

They could see his teeth. Those
looked even sharper.

Suddenly the door opened.
William was shaking a duster.

"Atchooo!" the cat sneezed.

25

"Eeeeek!" William squeaked.
He tried to run, but…

"Meeow!"

The cat pounced.

"Help!" shouted William. "Help!"

Mimi rushed towards the cat.
"Let go of my brother!"

"Hisssss!" The cat let go of
William.

"You're a big bully!" roared
Mimi.

The cat looked at her.

"A big bully, eh?" he said.
"Well, big bullies need dinners.
And you'll make a tasty –
yerrow! My tail!"

The cat leapt into the air. Ferdie grabbed Mimi and pushed her through the door. William rushed after them, and Ferdie shut the door with a slam.

Ferdie and Mimi stared at William.

William was picking fur out of his mouth.

"William!" said Ferdie. "Did you just bite the cat?"

William nodded.

"That's my brother,"
said Mimi. "He always does
things quietly."

"There," said the mouse. "See how clever mice are?"

"I don't know about that," said the rabbit. "Rabbits are very clever, you know."

"Woof!" said the puppy. "I know a story about rabbits too. Do you want to hear it?"

The rabbit looked cross. "You said you were going to go to sleep"

"But I'm still not tired!" The puppy ran round his cage.

"Let him tell his story," said the oldest guinea pig. "It might wear him out."

"But a boy's coming here to the shop tomorrow to choose a pet," the rabbit said, "We need to look our best. We mustn't look tired."

"It's only a little story," the puppy said hopefully. "And it **is** about rabbits."

The rabbit sighed. "Very well then."

Middle Rabbit and the Cabbage Field

Big Rabbit, Middle Rabbit and Baby Rabbit lived with their grandma and grandpa in a burrow.

Big Rabbit was big enough to go to the cabbage field on his own, but Middle Rabbit and Baby Rabbit were too small.

"But I'm big," said Middle Rabbit. "I'm bigger than Baby Rabbit."

"You're not big enough to go out alone," said Grandpa. "Eat your carrots, and you'll grow."

Middle Rabbit ate his carrots.
"Am I big enough now?" he asked.

"Not quite," said Grandma.
"Eat your lettuce."

Middle Rabbit ate his lettuce. "Am I big enough now?" he asked.

"No," said Big Rabbit. "You're not as big as me. When you're as big as me then you can go to the cabbage field on your own."

"Oh," said Middle Rabbit.

Middle Rabbit ate his cabbage. He ate his celery tops. He ate his parsnips. He ate his turnips.

Then he went to see if he was as big as Big Rabbit. "Am I as big as you now?" he asked.

Big Rabbit patted Middle Rabbit's head. "No," he said.

Middle Rabbit ate his beetroot. He ate his onions. He ate his radishes. He even ate his spinach.
He ran to see if he was as big as Big Rabbit. "Am I as big as you now?" he asked.

Big Rabbit pulled Middle Rabbit's ears. "No," he said.

"Bother," said Middle Rabbit and he went to sit under a tree.

Baby Rabbit followed him. "It's no good," Middle Rabbit sighed. "I'll never be as big as Big Rabbit."

Pop!

Mole pulled himself out of his hole.

"Why, hello, Big Rabbit," he said. "And hello to you too, Middle Rabbit."

Middle Rabbit looked round. He couldn't see Big Rabbit anywhere.

"Where's Big Rabbit?" he asked.

"You're here," said Mole.

"No," said Middle Rabbit. "I'm Middle Rabbit."

"And I'm Baby Rabbit," said Baby Rabbit.

Mole began to laugh. "Silly me! It's because I haven't seen you for so long! You've both grown."

Middle Rabbit looked at Baby Rabbit. Baby Rabbit looked at Middle Rabbit. "Have we?" they asked.

Mole laughed again. "Yes!"

"Oh!" said the rabbits. "Thank you, Mole!" They skipped back to their burrow.

"Grandma! Grandpa! Big
Rabbit!" said Middle Rabbit.
"Mole thought I was Big Rabbit!
So can I go to the cabbage field
on my own?"

"But you're still smaller than
me," said Big Rabbit.

Grandpa smiled. "Middle Rabbit
will always be smaller than you,
Big Rabbit – until you're both
grown up. He keeps growing – but
so do you!"

Grandma looked at Middle Rabbit. "We didn't notice," she said. "You are a big rabbit. Tomorrow you can go to the cabbage field all on your own."

"Hurrah!" said Middle Rabbit.

"And can I go on my own as well?" asked Baby Rabbit.

"You're not quite big enough yet," said Grandpa.

"Oh," said Baby Rabbit and his ears drooped.

Middle Rabbit looked at Baby Rabbit. There was a tear on the end of Baby Rabbit's whiskers.

"I'll go to the cabbage field on my own tomorrow," Middle Rabbit said. "But I might be lonely if I go on my own *every* day." He looked at Grandpa and Grandma. "Is Baby Rabbit big enough to come with me?" he asked.

"I'll eat my spinach!" said Baby Rabbit.

And Grandpa and Grandma said "Yes!"

"That," said the rabbit, "is a
good story. I'm sure the boy
coming to choose a pet will want
a rabbit. I'll do my best bouncing
when he comes."

"We'll spin round our wheel,"
said the brown mouse.

"We'll run round in circles," said
the guinea pig. She looked at the
puppy. "Do you know a story
about a guinea pig?"

"Oh **yes**," said the puppy.
"Do you want to hear it?"

The rabbit stamped
his foot.

"We'll have droopy ears
tomorrow if we don't go to sleep!"

"That's not fair." The guinea pig
frowned. "You've had a story,
and so have the mice! We want
one too!"

"And then can we go to
sleep?" asked the rabbit.

"Yes!" said the guinea pig, and
the puppy began his story.

The Very Special Breakfast

There was once a guinea pig, and his name was Toffee. He lived with his mum and his dad and his sister, and he was fussy about his food.

"Come along, dear," said his mum. "Eat your breakfast."

"Don't like cabbage," said Toffee.

"Try some carrot," said his dad.

"Don't like carrot," said Toffee.

"You can have some of my peas," said his sister.

"Don't like peas," said Toffee.

"I want ice cream. And cake.
And chocolate biscuits."

"But ice cream and cake and
chocolate biscuits aren't good for
guinea pigs," said his dad.

"Don't care," said Toffee, and he pitter-pattered off to see what he could find.

Toffee went to see the dog.
"What do you eat for
breakfast?" he asked.

"Bones," said the dog.

"Don't like bones," said Toffee,
and he pitter-pattered away.

Toffee went to see the cat.

"What do you eat for breakfast?" he asked.

"Fish," said the cat.

"Don't like fish," said Toffee,
and he pitter-pattered away.

Toffee went pitter-pattering
down the path and out into the
world. He hadn't gone far when
he met a fox.

"Good morning," said the fox. "Where are you off to in such a hurry?"

"I'm looking for my breakfast," said Toffee. "What do foxes eat?"

The fox looked at Toffee, and he licked his lips. "All kinds of things," he said. "What do you like eating?"

"Ice cream," said Toffee. "And cake. And chocolate biscuits."

"Fancy that," said the fox. "That's exactly what I'm going to have! Why don't you come with me?"

"Yes please," said Toffee, and he pitter-pattered along with the fox.
When they reached the fox's den, the fox opened the door.

"Do come in," he said.

Toffee hurried inside, and three little fox cubs jumped up.

"Daddy Fox, Daddy Fox, did you bring us our breakfast?" they asked.

"Guess what, my dears," said Daddy Fox.

"This little fellow has come to have breakfast with us. He's come to have ice cream. And cake. And chocolate biscuits. Isn't that lovely?"

And he winked at his three little fox cubs. The three little fox cubs winked back.

"Yum yum yum!"

they said.

"Now," said Daddy Fox. "I'll go and fetch Mummy Fox, and then we'll all sit down to have breakfast together."

Toffee looked round.

"What are those?" asked Toffee.

"Feathers," said the first little
fox cub.

"Feathers?" said Toffee. He
began to feel uncomfortable.

"Our mum's been stuffing
pillows," said the first little
fox cub.

"Oh," said Toffee. He couldn't
see any pillows, but he could see
something else.

"What's that?" asked Toffee.

"Fur," said the second little fox
cub.

"Fur?" said Toffee. He began to
feel nervous.

"Our mum's been sewing a fur
coat," said the second little fox
cub.

"Oh," said Toffee. He couldn't see a fur coat, but he could see something else.

"Oh!" Toffee stared, and his teeth began to chatter. "W ... w ... what are those?"

"Bones!" said the littlest fox cub. "Yum yum yum!"

"Ssh!" said his brothers.

It was too late. Toffee jumped up and ran.

The three little fox cubs chased after him calling "Come back! Come back!"

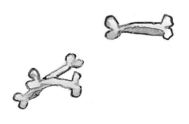

Toffee didn't stop. He ran and he ran and he ran all the way back home. He rushed through the door, and he slammed it shut.

"You're back," said his mum.

"Yes," said Toffee. "And I'm hungry. But I don't want ice cream. Or cake. Or chocolate biscuits. Can I have cabbage? And carrots? And peas? Please?"

"Toffee was silly," the guinea pig said. "I'd **never** eat ice cream."

The puppy didn't answer. He was curled in a ball, fast asleep.

"Thank goodness for that," said the rabbit. He yawned. "Let's hope he doesn't wake up too early!"

But the puppy slept on and on and on ...

When the boy came to the
pet shop in the morning, the
puppy was still asleep. The rabbit
bounced. The mice spun round in
their wheel. The guinea pigs ran
round in circles.

"Dear me," said the boy's
mother. "They look very full of
beans! I think I'd like a nice quiet
pet."

"Look at that little puppy," said
the boy. "He looks very quiet."

Mr Peter nodded. "Been
asleep all morning," he said.

The boy's mother smiled. "In that case, yes. We'll have the puppy."

"Hurrah!" said the boy. "Come on, puppy! Wake up!"

"Woof!" said the puppy.

As the boy, his mother and the puppy left the pet shop, the rabbit sniffed loudly. "Huh! They're in for a surprise. Now, nobody talk to me. I'm going to go to sleep."

And he did.

*Look out for more Early Readers
by Vivian French and Selina Young:*

The Kitten with No Name
ISBN 978-1-4440-0078-8
£4.99

Down in the Jungle
ISBN 978-1-4440-0513-4
£4.99

A Creepy Crawly Story

ISBN 978-1-4440-0515-8

£4.99